JPIC
Pras
W9-BJE-347
T. Veg : the story of a
carrot-crunching dinosaur
$16.95
ocn966314770

For every child who dares to be different,
and for Mel and Rob, with love – S.P-H.

For my students – K.M.

Cataloging-in-Publication Data has been applied for and may be obtained from the Library of Congress.

ISBN 978-1-4197-2494-7

Text copyright © 2017 Smriti Prasadam-Halls
Illustrations copyright © 2017 Katherina Manolessou
First published by Frances Lincoln Children's Books in 2015.

Copyright © Frances Lincoln Limited.

Printed and bound in China

10 9 8 7 6 5 4 3 2 1

Abrams Books for Young Readers are available at special discounts
when purchased in quantity for premiums and promotions as well as fundraising or
educational use. Special editions can also be created to specification.
For details, contact specialsales@abramsbooks.com or the address below.

ABRAMS The Art of Books
115 West 18th Street, New York, NY 10011
abramsbooks.com

T. VEG

THE STORY OF A CARROT-CRUNCHING DINOSAUR

WORDS BY
SMRITI PRASADAM-HALLS

PICTURES BY
KATHERINA MANOLESSOU

Abrams Books for Young Readers • New York

REGINALD THE T. REX HAD
A FIERCE AND MIGHTY
ROAR!

HIS FIERCE AND MIGHTY
FOOTSTEPS THUNDERED THROUGH
THE JUNGLE FLOOR.

HE RAN AS FAST
AND LEAPED AS FAR
AS ANY T. REX COULD.

HE STOMPED ABOUT
AND **GNASHED**
HIS TEETH AS EVERY T. REX SHOULD.

HE JUST HAD ONE SMALL WORRY,
ONE TEENY, TINY THING . . .
AT DINNER TIME HE OFTEN FELT
THAT HE DID NOT FIT IN.

FOR WHILE THE OTHER T. REXES
MUNCHED ON JUICY STEAK . . .

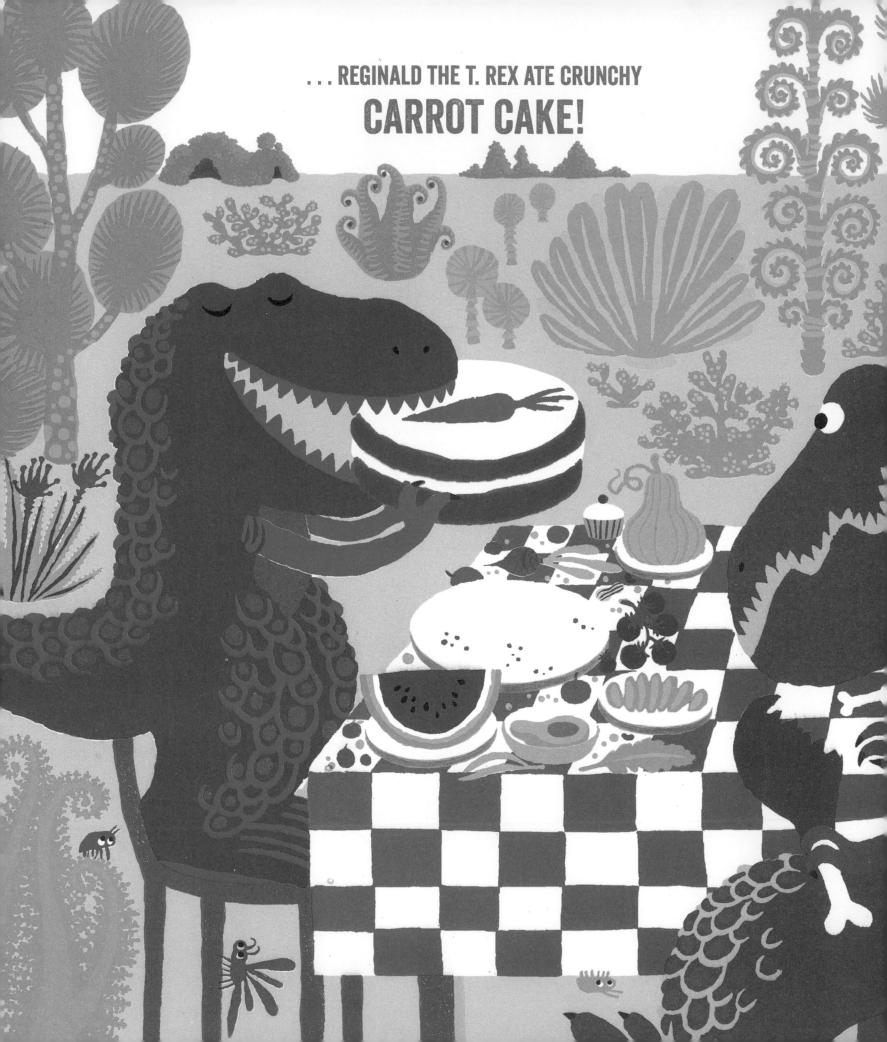

REGINALD ATE **BROCCOLI**, REGINALD ATE **BEANS**.
REGINALD ATE BOWLS AND BOWLS OF **GARLIC**, **GRAPES**, AND **GREENS**.

"IT'S JUST SO YUM!" HE TOLD HIS FRIENDS. "YOU MUST GIVE THIS A TRY," WHILE WOLFING DOWN A MASSIVE SLICE OF **AVOCADO** PIE.

MANGOES, PEACHES, PINEAPPLES, HE ATE THEM BY THE DISH.

"BANANA-BERRY SHAKE," HE'D SAY. "MMM, THAT'S SO DELISH!"

CARROTS, PARSNIPS, LETTUCES . . . OH YES, HE ATE THEM, TOO!
AND FOR A TEATIME TREAT HE MUNCHED ON PEA AND SPINACH STEW.

"FOR GOODNESS' SAKE WHAT'S WRONG WITH YOU?"

PAPA T. REX GROANED.

"YOU SHOULD BE EATING

MEAT,

MEAT,

MEAT!"

MAMA T. REX MOANED.

"YOU'LL NEVER WIN THE TYRANNOLYMPICS!"
LAUGHED HIS BEST FRIEND, HUGH.

"WHY EVER NOT?" ASKED REGINALD. "I'M JUST AS FAST AS YOU."

AT SCHOOL THE OTHERS ALL POKED FUN. THEY DIDN'T UNDERSTAND.
"THERE'S NEVER BEEN A VEGETARIAN T. REX IN THIS LAND!"

"T. REXES NEED LOTS OF MEAT,
IT'S THAT WHICH MAKES US STRONG.
AND IF YOU'RE EATING VEGETABLES,
YOU'RE DOING IT ALL WRONG!"

"HO HO HO," AND "HA, HA, HA," THEY LAUGHED AT POOR OLD REG.
"YOU'RE NOT A T. REX AFTER ALL . . .
TYRANNOSAURUS VEG!"

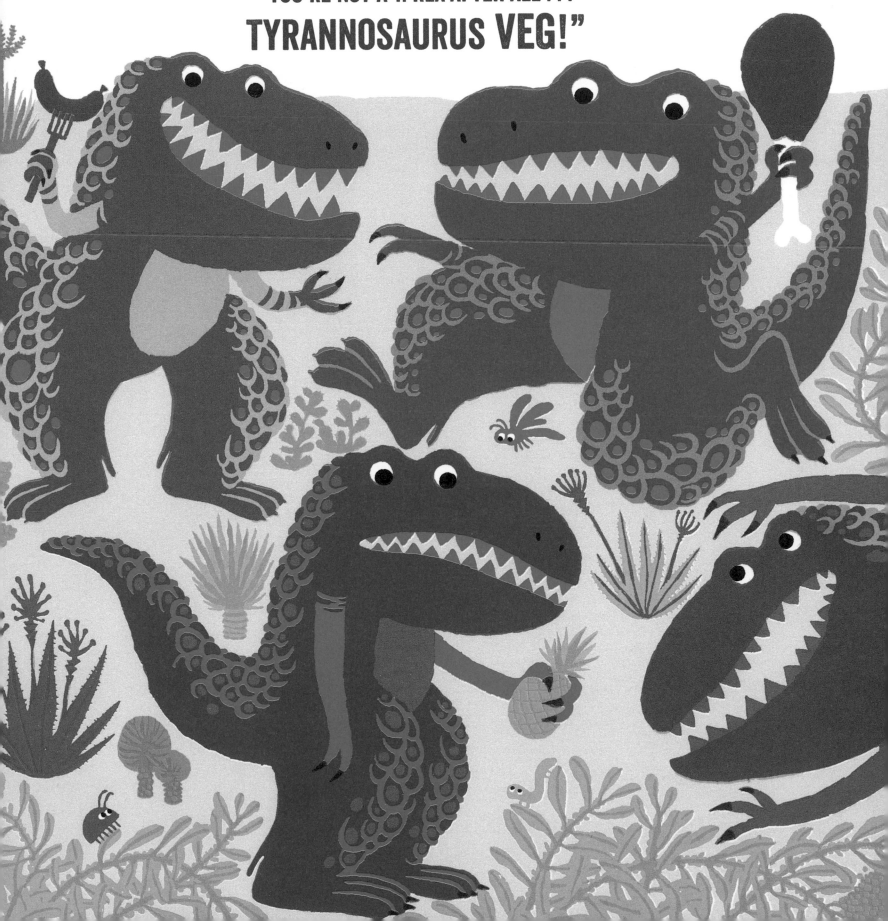

SO, FEELING RATHER MISERABLE, REG PACKED HIS DINO-SACK.
"GOOD-BYE! I'M LEAVING HOME," HE CALLED, "AND **NEVER** COMING BACK!"

"I WANT TO FIND SOME BETTER FRIENDS WHO'LL UNDERSTAND ME MORE.
THE TRUTH MIGHT BE THAT ACTUALLY I AM A HERBIVORE!
I'LL TRY AND DO SOME HERBIE THINGS. IT WILL BE FUN I BET . . ."

BUT STANDING DEEP IN RIVER SLIME WAS

HORRID,

COLD,

AND WET!

HE TRIED TO DO SOME **MOOING** BUT IT SOUNDED JUST LIKE ROARING,

AND SLOWING TO A GENTLE JOG WAS JUST A LITTLE **BORING**.

AND WHEN IT CAME TO **FORAGING**, REG DIDN'T HAVE A CLUE.
"I'D BETTER FIND SOME HERBIVORES TO SHOW ME WHAT TO DO!"

"WHAT LUCK!" CRIED REG. A GROUP OF THEM WERE GRAZING JUST AHEAD. HE STARTED STOMPING FASTER. "I'LL MAKE FRIENDS WITH **THEM**," HE SAID. BUT AS HE CHARGED TO GREET THEM AND WAS STILL QUITE FAR AWAY . . .

THE HERBIES TOOK ONE LOOK AT REG . . .

AND **SHRIEKED**
AND **RAN AWAY!**

MEANWHILE AT HOME THE T. REXES WERE MISSING T. REX REG.
"SO WHAT IF HE ATE FRUIT?" SAID HUGH. "SO WHAT IF HE ATE VEG?
THERE'S NO ONE WHO CAN STOMP LIKE HIM, OR PLAY OUR T. REX GAMES.
WE **HAVE** TO GO AND FIND HIM QUICK AND BRING HIM HOME AGAIN."

OFF THEY SET, BUT PRETTY SOON THEY HEARD A DISTANT RUMBLE. THE CLIFF TOP RIGHT ABOVE THEIR HEADS BEGAN TO CREAK . . . CREAK . . . CRUMBLE.

A MASSIVE ROCK WAS SLOWLY CRASH . . .

CRASH . . .

CRASHING

DOWN THE HILL.

THE T. REX CLAN WAS SURE THEY WOULD BE CRUSHED, THAT WAS, UNTIL . . .

REGINALD THE T. REX SPOTTED THEM FROM FAR AWAY.

HE GALLOPED TO THEIR RESCUE AND HE BRAVELY SAVED THE DAY!

HE PUSHED WITH ALL HIS MIGHT AND STOPPED THE BOULDER WITH HIS WEIGHT.

HE HELD IT BACK AND SET THEM FREE BEFORE IT WAS TOO LATE.

THE T. REX CREW WAS SO AMAZED.

"HURRAH FOR **T. VEG REG!**
YOU'RE JUST SO **STRONG!**"

"OH YES," REG LAUGHED.
"IT'S ALL MY
FRUIT AND **VEG!**"

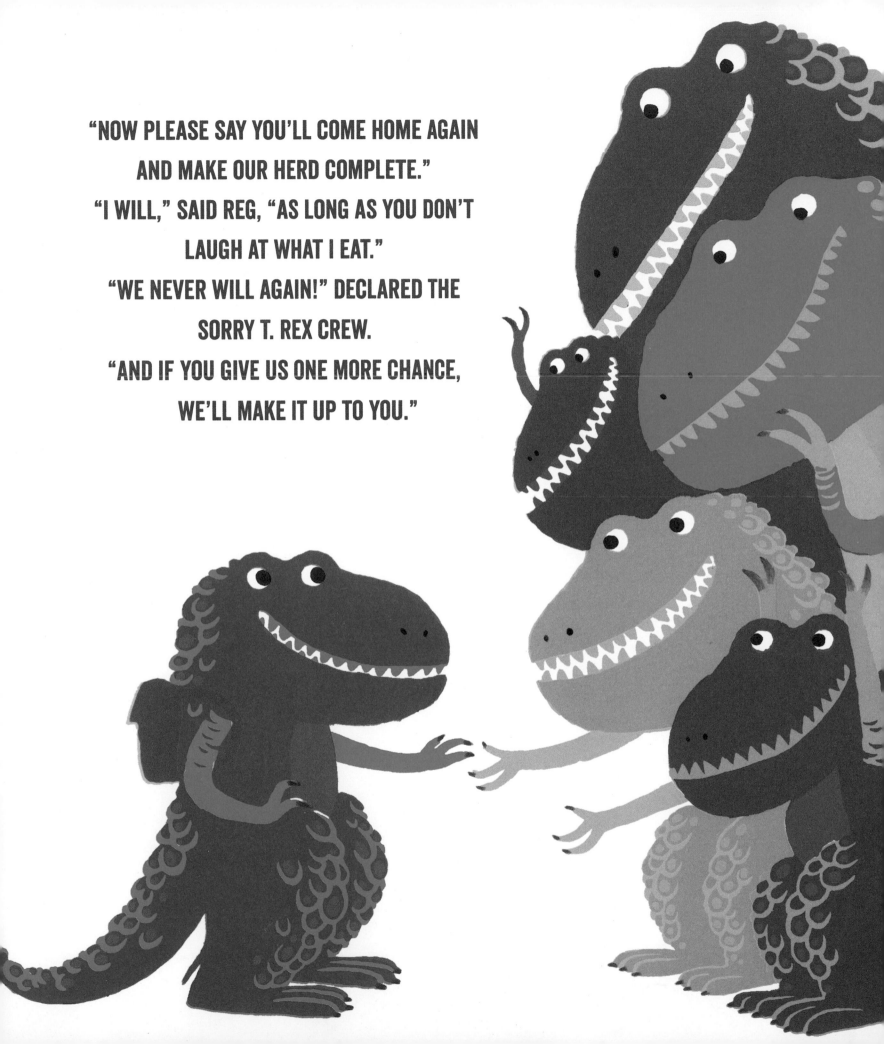

"NOW PLEASE SAY YOU'LL COME HOME AGAIN
AND MAKE OUR HERD COMPLETE."
"I WILL," SAID REG, "AS LONG AS YOU DON'T
LAUGH AT WHAT I EAT."
"WE NEVER WILL AGAIN!" DECLARED THE
SORRY T. REX CREW.
"AND IF YOU GIVE US ONE MORE CHANCE,
WE'LL MAKE IT UP TO YOU."

AND SO THE DINOS COOKED A **FEAST** OF VEGETABLE KEBABS,
AND ROASTED SQUASH AND MUSHROOMS,
WHICH THEY ALL AGREED WERE **FAB**!

AND THEN THEY DANCED THE NIGHT AWAY,
BECAUSE THEY **KNOW** IT'S TRUE . . .
THE BEST THING IN THE WORLD IS BEING HAPPY BEING **YOU!**